Our Emotions and Behavior

I Hate Everything!

Sue Graves

Illustrated by
Desideria Guicciardini

ree spirit

Last night, Sam couldn't sleep because Charlie was **crying.**

Sam got mad. He **hated** it when Charlie cried.

In the morning, Sam wanted to play soccer with Dad. But Dad was **busy.**

Dad said he would play later.
Sam wanted Dad to play now.
He got mad.

At lunchtime, Dad gave Sam some carrots. But Sam **hated** carrots. Dad said they would make him **big and strong.**

Sam said he didn't want
to be big and strong **ever!**
He got **very angry.**

Dad told Sam to go to his room
to **calm down.**

6

But Sam didn't want to go to his room.
He **didn't want to calm down.**

7

In the afternoon, Sam went to Archie's party. He wanted the piece of cake with the cherry on top, but Ellie took it.

Sam got **mad.** He **pushed** Ellie so hard she dropped her cake.

Then everyone played "Musical Chairs."
When the music stopped, Sam wasn't
fast enough. He didn't get a chair.
Archie said Sam was **out.**
Sam said he **wasn't out** at all.

"I hate everything!" Sam shouted.
He stamped his feet.
Everyone was **mad** at Sam
for **spoiling** the party.

Aunt Meg took Sam outside. She said when **she** felt angry she took a **deep breath** and counted slowly to ten.

Sam took a **deep breath.** He counted **slowly** to ten. Soon, he started to feel better. He didn't feel so mad anymore.

Aunt Meg told Sam there were lots of other things he could do when he felt **mad.** Sam thought about what he could do.

He said he could **read a book** ... or **tell someone** ... or **run** around the yard ... or **play** with his dog, Monty. Aunt Meg said these were all good ideas.

Sam wished that he had not spoiled
Archie's party.

He told everyone he was SORRY.

Then everyone played "Hide and Seek."
Everyone ran and hid. Archie counted
to **ten.**

Then he looked . . . and looked . . . and the first person he found was **Sam!** And Sam . . .

didn't get **mad** at all!

Can you tell the story of what happens when Owen has to have his hair cut?

How do you think Owen felt before he had his hair cut? How did he feel afterward?

A note about sharing this book

The **Our Emotions and Behavior** series has been developed to provide a starting point for further discussion about children's feelings and behavior, in relation both to themselves and to other people.

I Hate Everything!
This story explores in a reassuring way some typical situations that people dislike. It demonstrates how to cope in such situations and how to interact successfully with others.

The book aims to encourage children to have a developing awareness of behavioral expectations in different settings. It also invites children to begin to consider the consequences of their words and actions for themselves and others.

Picture story
The picture story on pages 22 and 23 provides an opportunity for speaking and listening. Children are encouraged to tell the story illustrated in the panels: Owen thinks he hates having his hair cut, and he makes a big fuss. When he arrives at the salon, he is diverted by the idea of driving the car. In the end, he is pleasantly surprised to find that having a haircut can, in fact, be a fun experience.

How to use the book
The book is designed for adults to share with either an individual child or a group of children, and as a starting point for discussion.

The book also provides visual support and repeated words and phrases to build confidence in children who are starting to read on their own.

Before reading the story
Choose a time to read when you and the children are relaxed and have time to share the story.

Spend time looking at the illustrations and discussing what the book may be about before reading it together.

After reading, talk about the book with the children

- What was it about? What things do the children "hate"? How do they cope when they have to deal with something they don't enjoy? Encourage the children to talk about their experiences.

- Do the children dislike some similar things? Examples might be having to go to bed on time or having to eat all their vegetables. Encourage the children to talk not only about why they don't like doing these things, but also about why it is important that they do them.

- Extend this discussion by talking about other things that children "hate," such as trying new foods or new experiences. Have the children ever tried something and then changed their opinion? Point out that it is a good idea always to try something rather than decide that they hate it.

- Spend time talking to the children about other words they might use instead of *hate* when describing situations they dislike. Examples might be feeling annoyed at having to clean their bedrooms or having to entertain a younger brother or sister. They may feel afraid of dark places or uncomfortable or anxious around snakes or bees. Encourage the children to use new words to describe their feelings.

- Look at the end of the story again. Sam felt much happier when he laughed about being found first in "Hide and Seek" instead of getting angry. Why do the children think Sam felt happier with this new attitude?

- Look at the picture story. Ask the children to tell the story in their own words. Why do they think Owen didn't want to have his hair cut? Do the children think he enjoyed the experience after all? Do they think he felt more comfortable after his haircut than before? Why? Do the children like having their hair cut? Why or why not? Again, encourage the children to talk about their own experiences.

- Ask the children to draw something they dislike and something they like very much. Encourage them to talk about their drawings during group time. Encourage them also to tell the others the strategies they employ to help them when they feel angry about something.

Published in North America by Free Spirit Publishing Inc., Minneapolis, Minnesota, 2013.

Library of Congress Cataloging-in-Publication Data (to come)
Graves, Sue, 1950–
  I hate everything! / Sue Graves ; illustrated by Desideria Guicciardini.
    pages cm. — (Our emotions and behavior)
  Audience: Age 4 to 8.
  ISBN-13: 978-1-57542-443-9
  ISBN-10: 1-57542-443-6
 1. Anger in children—Juvenile literature. I. Guicciardini, Desideria, illustrator. II. Title.
  BF723.A4G73 2013
  152.4'7—dc23

                                        2013012336

Reading Level Grade 1; Interest Level Ages 4–8; Fountas & Pinnell Guided Reading Level I

10 9 8 7 6 5 4 3 2 1
Printed in China
S14100513

Free Spirit Publishing Inc.
Minneapolis, MN
(612) 338-2068
help4kids@freespirit.com
www.freespirit.com

First published in 2013 by Franklin Watts, a division of Hachette Children's Books • London, UK, and Sydney, Australia

Text © Franklin Watts 2013
Illustrations © Desideria Guicciardini 2013

The rights of Sue Graves to be identified as the author and Desideria Guicciardini as the illustrator of this Work have been asserted in accordance with the Copyright, Designs and Patents Act, 1988.

Editor: Jackie Hamley
Designer: Peter Scoulding